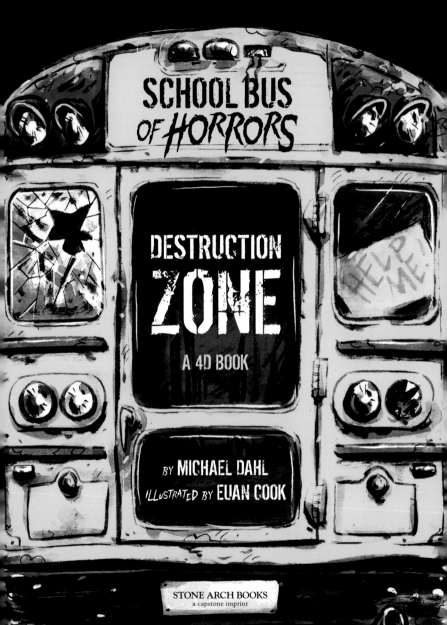

SCHOOL BUS
OF HORRORS

DESTRUCTION
ZONE

A 4D BOOK

BY MICHAEL DAHL

ILLUSTRATED BY EUAN COOK

STONE ARCH BOOKS
a capstone imprint

School Bus of Horrors is published by
Stone Arch Books
A Capstone Imprint
1710 Roe Crest Drive
North Mankato, Minnesota 56003
www.mycapstone.com

Cataloging-in-Publication Data is available at the Library of Congress website.
ISBN 978-1-4965-6267-8 (library binding)
ISBN 978-1-4965-6273-9 (paperback)
ISBN 978-1-4965-6279-1 (eBook PDF)

Summary: During a field trip, a school bus takes students on a detour due to road construction. Then another. And another! The bus seems to be driving in circles, as if the streets have become a giant maze. Will the students ever reach their final destination?

Designer: Bob Lentz
Production Specialist: Tori Abraham

Cover background by Shutterstock/Evannovostro

Printed in the United States of America.
PA021

Download the Capstone app!

- Ask an adult to download the Capstone 4D app.

- Scan the cover and stars inside the book for additional content.

When you scan a spread, you'll find
fun extra stuff to go with this book!
You can also find these things
on the web at www.capstone4D.com
using the password: zone.62678

TABLE OF CONTENTS

From dawn to dusk, the **SCHOOL BUS OF HORRORS** rumbles along city streets and down country roads, searching for another passenger. Yellow, black markings, dirty windows—it looks like any other.

But **BEWARE!** Step aboard this bus and experience the scariest ride of your life . . .

CHAPTER ONE
DEAD THINGS

"Who cares about a museum?" says Ivy.

She shakes her head, tossing her long braids.

"Especially a *doll* museum," she adds. "Talk about creepy!"

Ivy is standing in line to get on a bus.

Today is Field Trip Day.

"Hurry up, people," says her teacher, Mr. Hong. "We leave in five minutes."

Ivy rolls her eyes. "Boring."

Her friend, Gracie, snaps her gum. "Totally," she agrees.

Ivy steps onto the bus.

She is surprised that she can't see the driver.

The shadow of a man sits behind a plastic wall.

His voice comes through a few small holes in the barrier.

"I agree with you girls," says his whispery voice. "Who wants to see a bunch of dolls?"

Ivy and Gracie rush down the narrow aisle and quickly find a seat.

"Creepy," says Ivy.

"You said it!" says Gracie.

"Should we tell Mr. Hong?" asks Ivy.

A rumbling sound comes from under the floor.

The bus lurches forward.

Gracie looks around.

"He's not here," she says. "Maybe he's on the other bus."

CHAPTER TWO
THE CRASH

The bus zooms down the street. It strikes a trash can on the curb.

Ivy holds on to her seat and glances out the window.

"He's going too fast!" she says.

Other students around her start shouting.

A boy sitting at the front of the bus screams.

The driver steps on the brakes.

SCREEEEECH!

The bus turns sideways, skidding down the street.

Ivy and Gracie are thrown from their seat.

"Look out!" screams a boy.

"We're going to hit that building!" shouts Gracie.

CHAPTER THREE
THE WRONG LANE

The strange bus zooms down the street.

Ivy looks out the window.

"The driver is sure going fast," she says.

"Too bad," Gracie says. "I'm not in a hurry to get to that stupid museum."

Ivy remembers what the bus driver said. *Dolls. Who wants to see a bunch of dolls?*

The bus picks up speed.

"Excuse me, driver!" says Mr. Hong.

That's weird, thinks Ivy. *I thought Mr. Hong was on the other bus.*

"We just passed the museum!" Mr. Hong shouts.

Gracie points at the windshield.

"We're in the wrong lane!" she screams.

The driver steps on the brakes.

The bus turns sideways, skidding down the street.

The boy in the front seat screams.

The windshield shatters.

CHAPTER FOUR
THE SAME TRUCK

The bus zooms down the street.

Ivy turns in her seat and looks out the dirty window.

"It sure is taking a long time to get there," she says.

"Hey!" says a boy at the front. "The museum is back there!"

Gracie stands up in her seat.

"He's right," she says.

BRRRUMMMMMMPP!

The children fly out of their seats.

Ivy's braids smack against her face.

"Excuse me, driver," says Mr. Hong. "I think we just passed the museum!"

An icy fist grips Ivy's stomach.

"This has happened before," she says aloud.